TALES FROM
THE
PANCHATANTRA

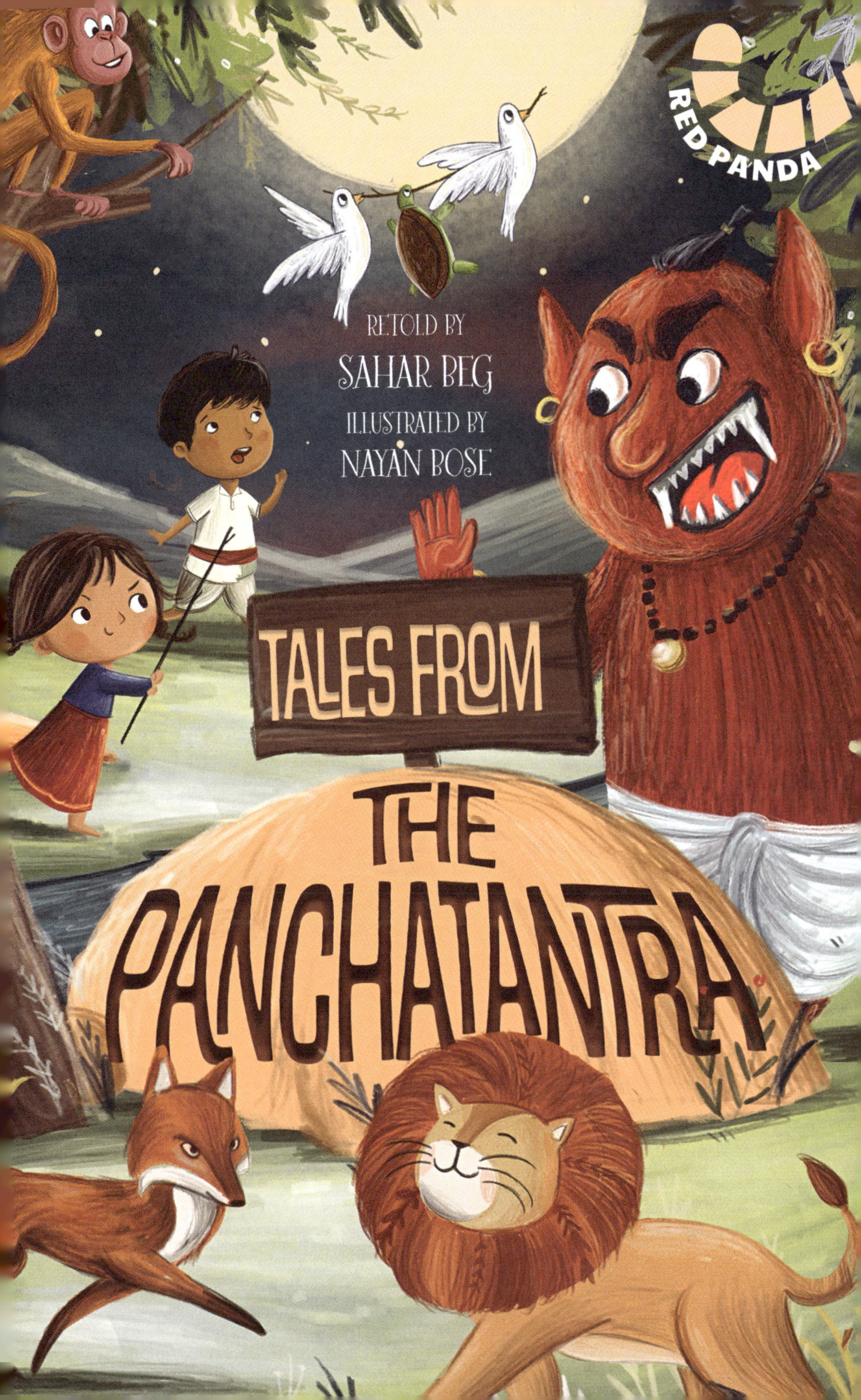
RED PANDA
RETOLD BY
SAHAR BEG
ILLUSTRATED BY
NAYAN BOSE
TALES FROM
THE
PANCHATANTRA

Published by Red Panda, an imprint of Westland Books, a division of Nasadiya Technologies Private Limited, in 2025

No. 269/2B, First Floor, 'Irai Arul', Vimalraj Street, Nethaji Nagar, Alapakkam Main Road, Maduravoyal, Chennai 600095

Westland, the Westland logo, Red Panda and the Red Panda logo are the trademarks of Nasadiya Technologies Private Limited, or its affiliates.

ISBN: 9789360458997

10 9 8 7 6 5 4 3 2 1

Book Design by Pratik M Kalekar

Printed at Thomson Press (India) Ltd

A long, long time ago—more than two thousand years back, in the third century BCE—there lived a wise scholar in ancient India named Vishnu Sharma. In those days, storytelling was one of the best ways to share ideas and Vishu Sharma had a special mission: he wanted to teach kings to govern wisely.

But instead of writing boring lessons, he had a brilliant idea. He filled his stories with talking animals—like cunning foxes, brave elephants and playful monkeys—along with clever and even foolish men and women who went on exciting adventures. Through their journeys, they taught valuable lessons on kindness, courage, friendship and wisdom.

And that's how *The Panchatantra* was born—a magical collection of fables full of fun and hidden wisdom, passed down through the ages. You might have heard some of these stories before, but this collection—retold by Sahar Beg and illustrated by Nayan Bose—invites a new generation of readers to enjoy them in a fresh way. These tales aren't here to lecture—they're here to enchant, entertain and gently guide.

So, open these pages and dive into this ancient realm of storytelling, where every tale has a secret to share and every creature has something to say. Let the adventure begin!

CONTENTS

1. THE RISE AND FALL OF THE MERCHANT

In a rich and flourishing kingdom, there lived a merchant who worked in the king's court. He was a sharp and diplomatic man who soon caught the king's eye. As an efficient worker and a problem solver, he was fairly popular in court. All these traits led to him often being favoured by the king.

When the merchant's daughter was married, he held a lavish reception where he invited not just the king and the queen but the entire royal household as well as many respected and influential people from the kingdom.

It was a happy and joyous day for him and his family. He spent most of the day running around, making sure all his guests were comfortable. At one point, he saw a man who worked as a servant at the palace, sitting in the seats reserved for the king and queen. Feeling stressed, he unthinkingly ordered him to be removed from the gathering entirely.

Humiliated, the servant returned to work the next day and kept an eye out for the merchant. When he saw how much the king seemed to like him, he began to think of a way to get back at him. But what could he, a servant, do that would harm such a well-liked and respectable man?

When he was cleaning the king's room a few days later, he

noticed that the king was not yet fully asleep. As he began to sweep near the bed, he muttered to himself, 'That merchant has become too forward. To embrace the queen like that!'

This made the king sit up in bed.

'What did you just say? Who embraced the queen?'

The servant bowed his head and answered softly, 'Oh, my king, please pay me no attention. It's only that I thought I saw the merchant ... but no, I must be wrong. I haven't been sleeping well—I must have simply misunderstood something.'

But a seed of doubt had been planted in the king's mind. As he sat on his throne the next day, he kept a close watch on the merchant. The servant's job took him all over the palace, just as the merchant's did. What if he really had seen something? The king found himself overthinking the merchant's every move. When he saw him greet the queen by taking her hand with a bow, he couldn't take it anymore.

Suddenly, the next morning, the merchant found that he was no longer allowed in the palace! He stood at the gates, arguing with the guards, trying to explain that he had been part of the king's court for years. But no matter what he said the guards refused to let him in.

Just at that moment, the servant happened to be passing by and couldn't help but make a comment.

'Be careful! That man will have you losing your jobs if you don't do as he asks,' he called out to the guards.

The merchant looked at him and slowly realised where he had seen him before. He knew the servant must have said something to ensure he wouldn't be allowed in—as payback for being kicked out. He went home dejected and tried to think of a way to fix the mess he had made.

He decided to try to make it up to the servant. He invited him to his house and treated him like an esteemed guest.

He talked to him with great respect and even served him personally. When they had finished eating, he tried to explain his past actions.

'Please do not think I removed you from my house because I consider myself better than you. It was just that you were sitting in the seats reserved for the king and queen. I had never hosted royalty before and was already quite nervous. I apologise if you felt insulted.'

Rarely had the servant been treated so well. He was deeply flattered and forgave the merchant at once.

'It means a lot that you would go to such lengths for me. I can understand why the king favours you. I will do my best to make sure that it remains that way, for today, you have found a friend in me.'

The next day, while cleaning the king's room, the servant once again started muttering to himself.

'The king is such a strange man—I hear he eats while going to the bathroom.'

Again, the king sat up upon hearing what the servant was saying.

'What nonsense are you spewing! Where have you heard all this?' he demanded.

'My lord, forgive me! I was up late again and don't know what I'm saying. Please pay me no attention,' the servant said, falling to his knees.

The king knew for a fact he had never eaten in the bathroom. Just the thought of it made him uncomfortable. This servant was clearly not in his right mind. But that meant that what he had said about the merchant couldn't be trusted either. And really, now that he thought about it, the merchant hadn't done anything suspicious.

The king feared he had made a terrible mistake. How could

he have let a few stray words make him doubt someone he had trusted for years?

With this in mind the king summoned the merchant back to the palace. He bestowed a great many gifts upon him and reinstated his position in the court. Everyone was overjoyed to see him back. Both the royal and city affairs had suffered in his absence.

The merchant and servant greeted one another warmly every time they saw each other in the palace, knowing they had found a friend in one another.

2. THE MONGOOSE AND THE SNAKE

Once upon a time, in a warm and cozy house, there lived a small family. The mother, father and their baby spent their days content and happy with their simple life.

One quiet day, while the father was out working in the fields, he found a baby mongoose. He looked all around but could not find its mother. Knowing the tiny creature wouldn't survive on its own while it was so young, he decided to take it home.

His wife was very alarmed when she saw what he had brought home. She was worried that their baby wouldn't be safe with a mongoose in the house. But once she realised how young and defenceless the small animal was, she began to pity it. She did not want to be the reason for its death.

So the mongoose and baby grew up together. As the days went by, the mother, too, got used to having him around and was no longer fearful. With plenty to eat and a safe place to rest, the mongoose became big and strong in just a few months. He would often spend his days by the baby's side, playing and keeping her company. They became very fond of each other.

One day, as the father was getting ready to leave for work, he discovered that they were out of water.

'Can you go and refill our water today? The matka is completely empty,' he said to his wife.

'If you wait with the baby, I can go do it right now,' she responded.

But the father was already running late and couldn't wait any longer. He insisted that the baby would be fine for the twenty minutes she would be gone, especially since the mongoose would be with her.

'Are you sure you can't wait until I come back? I don't want to leave the baby alone,' the mother said.

'But she's not alone. We have the mongoose to watch over her,' the father replied cheerfully.

The mother was not convinced. If something happened, she would never be able to forgive herself. But her husband seemed so confident, and she herself had seen the mongoose trail after her baby all day, making sure she didn't run into anything. Plus, she wasn't going to be gone for long; the water pump was fairly close to their house.

So, she and her husband set off on their respective tasks for the day, trusting the baby with the mongoose.

The baby had been settled down for her nap, and the mongoose was curled on the ground by her bed. At a glance, one would think that he was fully relaxed, settling down and letting out a small puff of air. However, he was completely aware of his surroundings.

After a few minutes, the mongoose suddenly tensed. As he lifted his head off the floor, he noticed a snake across the room. Snakes and mongooses are born enemies. Moreover, the mongoose was also very protective of the baby.

The mongoose leapt up and attacked the snake. He caught it between his teeth and they thrashed on the ground. The snake began coiling tightly around the mongoose too. Both animals were incredibly powerful in their own ways, making it a brutal fight. In the end, however, it was the mongoose's fierce protectiveness and determination that prevailed. He bit down on the snake's neck. After a moment of struggling, the snake went still.

Half an hour later, the mother was nearing home. Her footsteps were a little faster than usual, the payal on her ankles tinkling as she hurried back. She knew she was being paranoid; she hadn't been gone long enough for anything to have happened.

At the front door, the mongoose sat waiting. He was so proud of having protected the home and the baby. He couldn't wait for the mother to see how well he had done.

However, as soon she reached the door and saw the mongoose's face, she screamed. It came from deep within her and tears flooded her eyes. There sat the mongoose with blood all over his mouth. How could she have been so foolish? He had attacked her baby! Without thinking, she hurled the matka full of water on the unsuspecting mongoose.

CRASH!

Panicked, she ran into her house. What she saw inside sent a chill throughout her body. There lay her baby, safe in her bed, crying after hearing her mother scream. And in the corner lay a dead snake.

She ran to her baby and held her in her arms, rocking her. She closed her eyes for just a second. Then, she stepped outside again, to where the mongoose lay deathly still. She crouched with the baby tucked against her chest with one arm. Even as she brushed the broken matka pieces away from the mongoose's body, she knew it was too late. Her matka had been heavy and she had thrown it with such force that everything she feared had come true.

She stood there heartbroken and horrified. How was it that despite loving the mongoose with all her heart, she had not been able to trust his nature?

She would carry the memory of the mongoose for the rest of her life. It would guide her actions and the way she treated all the people and creatures in her life, trusting their actions and character, rather than her own biases.

3. THE SPARROW AND THE MONKEY

A twittering little sparrow had just finished building her nest on a high branch of a tree. She could not be more proud of her little home. She had worked tirelessly day and night, selecting only the best twigs and grass to build her nest.

She would feel a little flush of excitement at the end of each day at the thought of returning to her lovely nest. It would give her a little boost of energy after long days of flying in the sun.

The nest protected her from all kinds of weather. Whether it was hot or cold, rainy or dry, her nest remained a comfortable shelter.

One day, while the sparrow was out, it began to drizzle. She decided to return home early, which turned out to be a good idea as the soft drizzle soon turned into torrential rain.

She landed on the edge of her nest and began to shake off as much of the water from her feathers as she could. She fluttered her wings and shook her head before getting into her nest and settling in with a content sigh.

Looking out into the night, she watched as the heavy rain brought in a thunderstorm. Every few minutes, the world would

light up as lightning flashed across the sky, which was followed by a loud clap of thunder.

The sparrow was just about to tuck her beak into her wing and go to sleep when she heard a noise from the base of her tree. She looked down to see who could possibly be outside in such a fierce storm. This was a night best appreciated from the comfort and safety of one's home.

It took a while for her eyes to adjust in the darkness and pouring rain, but when they did, she saw a shivering monkey huddled on the ground. He was completely drenched, his teeth chattering as he tried to curl himself into a ball.

'Are you alright?' the sparrow called down at the monkey.

The monkey started and looked up. Catching sight of the sparrow, he scowled and said, 'What does it look like? I'm stuck in this miserable storm, aren't I?'

'Don't you have a place to take shelter? It would be horrible to have to wait out the storm like this. It doesn't look like it's going to stop anytime soon,' the sparrow said.

'Yes, thank you so much for pointing that out. Not everyone has a cozy little nest to hide in when things get rough,' the monkey replied, before looking away.

The sparrow looked at the monkey trying so hard to hide his trembling from the cold and felt a pang of pity. Perhaps she could offer him some advice to ensure he wasn't stuck in a situation like this in the future.

'You seem to have hands and feet like the humans do, and I have seen them build many things. I'm sure you could build yourself a lovely shelter if you tried.'

The monkey said nothing, refusing to even look in the sparrow's direction.

'I built my nest on my own too. It's not just something I found. It took a lot of work but I don't regret it at all. It's such a comfort to know you have someplace to go at the end of your day.'

She peered down at the monkey who was now trembling quite a bit. Still, he refused to look at her. Not giving up, she continued speaking.

'You'll understand what I mean when you have a place of your own. There's nothing like it. I'm surprised you didn't think of it yourself—you monkeys always seemed so smart.'

'You really think it's that simple, you arrogant bird?' the monkey finally spoke through gritted teeth.

'I don't mean to sound arrogant at all,' the clueless sparrow continued talking. 'If someone as small as me can do it with twigs and grass, then surely it shouldn't be so hard for you.'

'You should really shut up, you stupid bird. I just wanted someplace to wait out the storm, not some annoying chatterbox who thinks she's so smart.'

The sparrow was taken aback by the bitterness in the monkey's voice. He looked truly miserable, and she could not help but keep talking.

'You should take my advice, poor monkey. Here I sit, dry and comfortable while you are cold and wet. I can understand if you envy me, but take this as a lesson and be better prepared next time,' the sparrow said.

Hearing this was the monkey's last straw. He had been forced to listen to this bird gloat and preen from her warm little nest while he stood out in the storm. She thought she was much smarter than he was and kept throwing it in his face. Not able to hold back his anger anymore, he began to climb up the tree.

Seeing the monkey approach her with such a menacing look on his face, the sparrow grew alarmed. She chirped in fear and flew off her nest just as the monkey lunged for the branch.

In a rage, the monkey ripped the nest right off the tree. The sparrow watched in horror as he crushed her home in his palm, bits of it floating to the ground.

Breathing heavily, he yelled up at the bird, 'There! Now leave me in peace!'

The sparrow flew out into the storm, her heart pounding. The wind threw her in every direction before she was able to land on the branch of a nearby tree. Cold and shaking, she tucked herself into its leaves and waited for the storm to pass.

Both the monkey and the sparrow had a long night ahead of them. The monkey forgot the sparrow soon after the storm, but the sparrow remembered that encounter for a long time. She rebuilt her nest in a quiet tree and never again offered solutions where they were not requested.

4. THE THIEF AND THE MEN WITH JEWELS

Our story begins when three well-travelled and knowledgeable men came to a town that was home to a thief. The men had wares to sell during the day and stories to share in the evening.

They had the entire town charmed with their wild and exotic tales of adventure. Every day, more and more people came to them to buy their wares. They had things from the many places they had visited. Balms for headaches, sprains, sore throats, clear throats, wounds of all shapes and sizes—they could solve problems you hadn't even heard of!

The thief watched as their supplies dwindled and riches grew. He began to dream of stealing all their money for himself and living comfortably for the rest of his days.

He began to go to them regularly and ask about their many experiences. He charmed them with stories of his small-town life and dreams of making it big one day. He expressed awe at their stories, flattering them at every opportunity. Finally, he asked if, maybe, he could travel with them to their next destination. The men agreed instantly.

Once they had sold all their wares, they began to make plans to leave. They had managed to make a fair bit of money

here and didn't feel safe travelling with it. So they decided to buy jewels and carry those with them instead. They cut open their thighs and hid them there, using a balm to heal the cuts. They did not even think to hide all this from the thief, who was the only one who knew where all their riches were hidden.

Once they had all set off and left the town behind, the thief began to plan how he would rob them. He could poison them and take the jewels in the middle of the night. The roads they travelled were fairly deserted and offered the perfect opportunity for him to get away.

However, before he could do anything of the sort, they were confronted by a large group of bandits. The bandits had heard from the townsfolk that a group of traders who had sold all their wares were passing by. The bandits knew they would be rich and were determined to steal their wealth.

They captured the men and the thief and searched them thoroughly. They were patted down and had every pocket turned out. When the bandits found nothing, the leader turned towards them and began to threaten them.

'Don't think for a second that you all will be getting away. If you don't tell us where you've hidden the money, we have no problem looking everywhere till we find it. If you have swallowed it all, I will cut open your stomach to get to it.'

By now, the thief and the men had begun to tremble in fear. Their deaths seemed inevitable. The thief knew that if the bandits really did search their bodies, they would discover the jewels. No one would believe him if he told them that he was the only person who wasn't hiding anything. They would kill him regardless.

The thief looked at his fellow travellers and remembered how open they had been, not just with him but everyone in town. Now they looked scared and hopeless. He was going to die either way—shouldn't he at least try to save these people who had done no wrong?

He took a deep breath, gathering every bit of strength he possessed, before turning to the leader of the bandits.

'Please don't make me witness my friends' deaths! If you are going to kill us, I beg that you kill me first,' he cried.

'Ah, I see you have finally given up. A wise choice,' the bandit said.

'Yes, I cannot take this any longer. You can search me everywhere as much as you wish, you will discover nothing. I simply ask that you at least spare me the heartbreak of witnessing my friends' pain,' the thief said.

The bandits took him aside and searched him thoroughly. They slit open his thighs, his stomach and his arms. They looked everywhere and found no sign of any hidden money or jewels.

The bandits were confused and embarrassed. They had never made a mistake like this before. They untied the rest of the captured men and let them go.

As the men fled from the bandits, they sent up a prayer of gratitude for the sacrifice of their fallen companion. If not for him, none of them would be alive right now.

5. THE PRINCESS AND THE SNAKE PRINCE

There once lived a prince with a snake in his stomach. Everything the prince ate, the snake would eat as well. The prince grew weak and lived in constant pain. Doctors and healers of all kinds were called by the king to heal his son. They were all unsuccessful.

The prince felt he was a burden on his parents, and every luxury they offered brought him no comfort from the pain. One day, he decided to leave his kingdom behind and move to another land.

He finally decided to settle in a temple and live a humble life. He survived on other people's kindness and the alms they offered him.

This new kingdom was ruled by a king who had two daughters. The princesses were his pride, and he had educated them well. They had been presented with only the finest things in life since the moment they were born. They were known throughout the land to be very intelligent.

Every morning the elder princess would greet her father saying, 'Your blessings are the reason for all my joy.' Hearing this, the youngest would retort, 'Our blessings are the product of our own actions.'

One day the king was in a foul mood. When the princesses greeted him that morning, he got angry hearing his youngest daughter's daily quip.

'How can you say such a disrespectful thing? You should be grateful to me. I have given you everything a person could desire from life,' he said angrily.

His daughter bowed her head and said, 'I do not mean to be ungrateful, Father. I only meant that accidents of birth aside, it is what we make of what we are given that truly matters in this world.'

This sent the king into a rage. He wanted to teach his daughter a lesson and ordered his guards to find the most ill-suited man for her to marry. It just so happened that the prince was begging outside the palace that day. The guards saw him and presented him before the king.

The princess and prince were soon married. Since they would be unable to live in the temple as a married couple, they decided to travel the kingdom together, looking for a place to call home. Their respect and fondness for each other grew as the days went by and they got to know each other. They soon grew to be happy and content in their marriage.

One hot day as they were travelling, the prince began to feel unwell. He had been getting weaker and could not walk for long stretches of time. The princess went to get them some food and water as he sat down in the shade of a tree to rest.

He lay down and dozed off as he waited for his wife to return. A snake lived in the anthill by the tree he was sitting against and it happened to come out just then. Hearing another snake, the one living in the prince's stomach became intrigued and came out through the prince's mouth.

'Why do you live inside this man?' asked the snake who lived in the anthill. 'What do you get from making his life miserable? If he happens to drink anything with mustard you will be doomed.'

Offended, the other snake responded, 'Who are you to judge me and what I choose to do with my life? It's not like your choices make much sense either. You guard two pots of gold you have no use for.'

'You are just jealous that I live comfortably with more gold than most people can dream of while you are stuck inside a man's dark stomach.'

'Do not speak to me as if you know my life! If anyone were to find out what treasures you guard, they will not hesitate to come after you. All they need to do is pour hot oil and you too will be no more! At least where I live I am protected from the harsh outside world.'

As the snakes continued to argue, they failed to notice that the princess had overheard their entire exchange. She had almost screamed when she saw the two snakes—one of them in her husband's mouth. However, when she realised they were talking, she had quickly hid to overhear their conversation.

Now that she knew how to get rid of both snakes, she immediately gave her husband some mustard soup. He soon became well and his strength began to return. By pouring hot oil over the anthill, she was able to kill the other snake too and get the pots of gold.

With the prince healthy, they returned to his kingdom. His parents were overjoyed to see their son well and remained forever grateful to the princess for healing him.

The gold they brought with them made the kingdom prosperous. The prince and princess went on to be great rulers who were beloved by their people.

6. THE SAGE AND THE UNWANTED MOUSE

There was once a very devout and spiritual sage. He had dedicated his life to working as a volunteer at his village temple. Nothing brought him peace quite like spending the day quietly tending to the upkeep of that building.

Since the work he did was unpaid, he would go into the village once a day to ask for food. The villagers were grateful for all the work he did at the temple and were happy to feed him. Most days he had more food than he could eat and would end up distributing it amongst the many struggling families living near the temple. He did his best to make them as comfortable as possible.

He would store the food in the temple at night before going out the next morning to offer it to the beggars outside. In return, the beggars would help where they could with the temple work.

One day while retrieving the stored food, the sage noticed something odd. The containers were open. Looking inside, he understood that a mouse had helped itself to a hearty meal!

The sage was frustrated, as this meant the leftovers had to be thrown out. He didn't want to risk spreading any diseases.

He was determined to find this mouse and get rid of it.

He hung the food up high the next day to ensure the mouse wouldn't get in. He spotted many little holes all over the temple but couldn't find the mouse. The whole day was wasted in the hunt, and when he went to check on the food he saw that the mouse had managed to get in anyway!

Frustrated and upset, he spent many days in vain trying to get rid of this mouse. Whenever he did catch sight of it, he was never fast enough to actually catch it. Many hours were spent fruitlessly trying to bait the mouse out of hiding.

On one such day, the temple happened to have a visitor. A beggar had walked from a long way away to visit this temple after hearing of the sage's generosity.

'I hear you feed all those who ask. I have come hoping to get a meal, as I have not eaten in many days.'

The usually attentive and helpful sage was distracted, as the mouse had evaded him once again. He didn't reply to the beggar at the door, who began to get offended.

'I was told that people here are exceptionally kind, but I find that the man in charge here cannot even answer my simple question!'

At this angry exclamation, the sage finally looked up. He felt embarrassed and flushed a little.

'No, no,' he apologised. 'Please come in and sit down. I'm so sorry. It's only that there is a mouse in the temple who has been troubling me for days now. But it is no excuse to leave a guest waiting at the door—I do apologise.'

Seeing how genuine the sage was, the beggar's anger faded.

'It's alright,' he said. 'I can understand. How long has this been going on?'

That was just the excuse the sage needed to rant about

this impossible mouse that had been haunting him for days. How he felt so terrible about not having enough food to give people as he used to. He had truly tried all that he could to get rid of the mouse and protect the food, but all his efforts seemed to be in vain. The mouse remained out of reach and always found the hidden food.

Hearing this, the beggar had an idea.

'With the amount of food that has gone missing, I think the mouse has been collecting and hiding it rather than eating it all. That would explain it's unusual amount of energy as well. If we can find its stash and dispose it, it won't be able to keep hunting down all your food.'

'You truly think so?' the sage asked. 'My life will become so much easier if you can help me get rid of this mouse.'

'Of course,' the beggar said. 'We must strike right at the source of its strength to truly get rid of it.'

Now that he was not facing this alone, the sage felt empowered. They both started to search for mouse tracks inside the temple. They tracked them all to many little openings all over the place but did not find the all the food the mouse had been storing. So they kept looking.

Finally, they found a hole that seemed bigger than the rest. As they got closer to it, they could hear the mouse's little chirps coming from inside.

They began to widen the opening by hacking at it until an arm could comfortably fit through. Then the sage reached in and cleaned it out, causing the mouse to scurry out in fear. Soon a small heap of stale food was emptied out of the mouse's hiding place and thrown away.

Not having its backup stash of food to rely on anymore, it became harder for the mouse to keep hunting. The sage had also been keeping the food in increasingly harder-to-reach places. Soon, the mouse became slower and the sage was able to catch and get rid of it.

This brought immediate relief and ease to the sage's life. He could once again give out food to all those who needed it. He could spend his days peacefully in the temple and not have to run after a food-stealing mouse.

The sage remained forever grateful to the beggar's good advice.

7. A POOR MAN'S DREAMS

There was once a man who lived a rather rough life. He had no family or friends to rely on and often had to beg for money. Every time he did have food, instead of eating it to feel full and be able to work and earn, he would store most of it for another day.

It was just that the potential of something was always so much greater than the reality. The thought of having money or food that could one day make him happy was a great comfort to the man. Actually starting the work of improving his life with what he had was much harder.

And so his days went by much the same as the last, until one day when someone generously gave him a whole pot of kheer. Someone in his neighbourhood had just had a baby and there was too much food at the celebration. The man accepted this gift gratefully and took it home.

This time was going to be different, he decided. He was going to ensure he used this kheer to its full potential. It was not going to go to waste. Upon reaching his house, he ate a bowl full of the delicious kheer before tying the pot and hanging it from his ceiling. Looking at it, he fell asleep.

His dreams that night were sweet like the kheer in his

belly. They were full of possibility and hope about every single thing that could change for him now.

If his village suffered a famine, he could sell his kheer for a good amount of money and buy goats. Those goats would give him milk, which he could turn into curd or more kheer! The goats would eventually have babies and he would be able to sell them and buy cows or bulls.

He would then become a delivery man, using the bulls to drive a cart through the village. He would build connections that way, and some rich man, impressed by his hard work and dedication, would marry his daughter to him.

They would live comfortably and happily in a house provided by his wife's father. He would go out to work, and she would stay at home, cooking, cleaning and taking care of the house. Once a month they would make kheer using the milk from his cows.

Soon his cows would have calves. They would make decent money by selling those off as well. He would have to work less, and they would soon have children of their own who would grow up and take care of them one day.

He began to dream of how well he would raise his children. They would be well-behaved and disciplined. They would treat him with great respect and seek his advice often.

People would be in awe of how well he had managed to build his life, all beginning with just a pot of kheer. They would look at his children and know they were a true reflection of him and his character.

His dream then shifted to how envious people would be and how they might be driven to steal from him. They wouldn't manage to fool him though. He would be ready.

He got caught up in thinking about how he would protect his family and fortune. He would have a stick and beat any thief who entered his home. He began to get excited, not realising he had begun waving his arms around—not just in the dream.

His flailing arm just so happened to go in the wrong direction and there was a sudden crash! Waking up from the sudden noise, it took a few seconds for his heart to calm down and his eyes to adjust to the darkness.

What he saw before him was a tragic mess. The pot of kheer lay broken on the ground—the kheer spilled everywhere. The excitement of his dream had bled into reality, ensuring that it would never come true.

And so, the man's days went on as before, with no famine to turn his non-existent kheer into a fortune for buying goats.

8. A MAN, A THIEF AND A DEMON

This story takes place in the house of a quiet and reserved old man. He lived alone after his family unfortunately passed away before him. His days were mostly spent in prayer and meditation. He led a simple life and tended to keep to himself. His community remained fond of him, as he was a gentle and reliable person.

Many families would leave their children with him during the day while they went to work. Knowing he was clear-headed, he was often asked for advice by the young folk trying to find their way in life. He treated them all with dignity and they would make sure to visit him, often joining him during his prayers.

One day this man caught the attention of a thief. The old man had just been gifted two healthy cows by a child he used to look after. The child was now grown up and doing well in life. He was married and running a small dhaba.

The cows were looked after very well by the old man. They were plump and happy creatures. It was them the thief was after. Thinking the old man wouldn't be much of a threat, he decided to steal them in the middle of the night.

It was an especially dark night as the thief made his way to the man's house. The house was secluded and built away from the road, making it eerie in the darkness. The crescent moon's faint light was made fainter by the heavy clouds in the sky.

The thief crept along, trying to not get spooked by the sound of the wind rustling through the trees. He almost screamed when he saw the thing that was suddenly blocking his way.

In the middle of the path stood a ferocious demon. His eyes felt as if they were looking straight into the depths of the thief's soul. He stood there trembling as the demon spoke to him.

'Who goes there? Who would dare to venture out on a night such as this?'

'I'm going to rob a man of his two cows!' was what fell out of the thief's mouth. He was so scared he did not even think to lie.

The demon was shocked and pleased at the truthfulness of the thief. He was used to people trying to trick and lie to him. Somehow they never thought that a demon, an expert in lies and tricks, would be able to see through them.

'Your transparency pleases me. I will come with you on your quest to acquire these cows. It is a worthy mission for a night like this.'

The thief was so surprised it took him a second to answer. 'Of course, please come with me. If you want, you could help yourself to the man who owns the cows.'

'Ah, the thought of that pleases me immensely. Come, let us go while the moon is still hidden.'

The thief and the demon made their way into the man's house. The thief went straight to the cows and began to untie them. The demon made his way to the sleeping man.

Seeing the demon looming above the man with his mouth

open, the thief began to whisper, 'Wait! Let me leave with the cows first.'

The demon frowned. 'Why should you get what you want first? I am a demon and much more powerful than you. You should make sure I get my wish before you fulfil yours.'

'Yes, but you see, if you eat the man first, he may wake up and start screaming. That may alert someone to come running and I will get caught,' the thief tried to explain.

This made the demon angry. 'How am I to know that your stealing the cows will not wake him up first? I do not know how efficient of a thief you are.'

'What? I am an incredible thief! No one has been able to catch me in the act,' the thief replied, a little offended.

Caught up in their argument, they did not realise when their whispers turned into shouts. Both were convinced that they were entitled to what they wanted first.

'I'm the one who brought you here! You should be grateful and ensure my theft is a success!' the thief said.

'I should be grateful? You are the one who should be grateful that I did not eat you the moment I saw you! Have you forgotten I am a demon?' the demon roared back.

All this commotion caused the man to wake up. He lay in bed for a moment wondering what had woken him, before he caught sight of the demon. He sat up with a loud scream.

'AAAAAAAHHHHHHHH DEMMMOOOONNNN!'

The thief and demon jumped, looking at the man in shock. It seemed they had both forgotten where they were in the heat of their argument.

The poor frightened man brought his palms together and began to pray. It took the demon a moment to notice what he was doing. Once he realised, he panicked and vanished in a puff to protect himself.

This night had not gone in any way the thief could have imagined. He stood frozen near the cows until he realised the man was now coming towards him with a laathi. He was almost relived, because this was something he knew how to react to.

He turned around and ran, ready to put this terrible night behind him.

9. FOUR UNLIKELY FRIENDS

Once upon a time, four unlikely friends—Deer, Mouse, Crow and Tortoise—met every day in a meadow deep in the forest. They were all different but never ran out of things to talk about. They spent hours together, knowing they could rely on each other for anything.

One morning, the friends gathered, but Deer hadn't arrived. After a while, Tortoise asked, 'Are you sure something's not happened to Deer?'

'Look, I'm sure everything's fine,' said Crow. 'But if you're worried, I can check.'

'Oh, would you? That would make me feel better,' said Tortoise.

Crow spread his wings. 'Anything for you, Tortoise. But I expect some delicious insects when I get back with Deer!'

Crow soared above, confident that Deer was just distracted by some fresh grass. Meanwhile, Tortoise and Mouse waited, trying to stay calm. They saw Crow returning, cawing worriedly.

'Deer's caught in a hunter's trap!' Crow exclaimed. 'I tried to help, but the rope is strong. We need to act fast!'

'Where is he?' asked Mouse.

'By the river, near the large rock,' Crow replied.

'Okay, I'll run ahead and start cutting the ropes. You carry Tortoise and meet me there,' said Mouse and they hurried off.

Mouse arrived first and began gnawing through the ropes. When Crow and Tortoise landed, Tortoise sat beside Deer while Crow perched above to keep watch. Just as Mouse was almost done, Crow yelled, 'The hunter is coming!'

'I'm going as fast as I can!' Mouse called back.

'Leave me here,' Deer said in a panic. 'I don't want you to get caught because of me.'

'Don't say that,' said Tortoise. 'Just lie still. We'll all get out of this.'

They sat quietly, watching Mouse work. As the hunter's footsteps grew closer, the last rope snapped and they ran. Crow soared into the sky, Mouse hid in the bushes and Deer dashed into the trees. But just when Tortoise was about to enter the river, the hunter spotted him and grabbed him in a rage.

The others watched in horror. But they weren't going to leave Tortoise behind. They quickly made a plan.

Along the path, Deer lay still where the hunter could find him. Delighted, the hunter dropped Tortoise and rushed to grab Deer.

As soon as Tortoise hit the ground, Mouse began freeing him. This net was smaller and soon Tortoise was free. Crow swooped down and flew him to safety while Mouse hid in a hole.

When the hunter reached Deer, he leapt up and ran into the trees. The hunter was startled and fell. By the time he got up, all that remained was a tattered net. Furious, the hunter went home empty-handed.

Deer, Tortoise, Crow and Mouse gathered in their meadow, grateful for each other.

10. A DOG ON YOUR SHOULDERS

On a long winding road between two villages walked a man with a goat on his back. He had gone to see a fair set up in his neighbouring village and his luck had managed to win him a goat there.

He was as happy as can be, whistling a little tune as he made his way home. It was a few hours' walk, and he wanted his goat to be in good health when he got home. That way, his family would be impressed and happy rather than upset about having to feed and care for something else. So he draped the goat on his shoulders as he journeyed back.

This road was known to have robbers and crooks, but the man had been making this journey since he was a child. His aunt was married into a family in the next village, and he would often go to visit her and her children. Therefore, he knew what shortcuts were actually traps and where robbers were most likely to attack travellers. He felt fairly confident nothing would happen to him, as nothing had ever happened before.

But the thing is, he had never carried a young, healthy goat on this path either. That was too priceless a thing for any crook to pass up. Once the crooks spotted the man with the goat, they decided not to let him get away. The goat looked healthy, and they were hungry. This might keep them fed for days.

They stayed hidden for a while, knowing they needed a good plan to trick this man into giving up his goat. When they felt they had a good plan, one of them jumped in the man's way.

'Hello, traveller. Can I ask why you are carrying a dog on your shoulders in such a strange way?'

The man scoffed. 'What's wrong with you? It is very clearly a goat. Don't be ridiculous and get out of my way.'

'If you say so,' the crook replied. 'It just looks incredibly like a dog to me. It was an innocent question.'

With that, he left the man to continue walking home. After about fifteen minutes of the man walking along, wondering how a person could mistake a goat for a dog, there was another man in his path.

This was a second crook, who asked him the same question as the first. 'Why are you carrying a dog on your shoulders? You know they can comfortably walk beside you, right?'

This upset the man even more.

'What is going on here? Can you not see, you foolish man? This is a goat I'm carrying! Go away, don't ask me stupid questions.'

The crook threw up his hands as a sign of peace. 'Don't worry, I didn't mean to bother you. I truly thought you were carrying a dog.'

This left the man confused. This time as he continued to walk, the man was questioning himself. Surely he would have known if he had won a dog instead of a goat. Hadn't the people at the fair clearly said that it was a goat? He couldn't seem to recall it very clearly, but yes ... it was a goat that he placed on his shoulders.

He continued to walk, his doubt growing with every step. He tried to brush it off but couldn't. Had he heard anyone

say it was a goat, or had he assumed? Maybe his eyesight was beginning to weaken and he hadn't noticed. Perhaps the people at the fair had been too polite to correct him on his assumption. Why would two people think he was carrying a dog?

With all these thoughts running through his mind, he barely noticed a third man walking towards him. He started a little when the stranger asked him a question.

'I'm so sorry, but I just wanted to ask, is your dog hurt? Is that why you are carrying him?'

The man stared at the stranger who was actually the third crook to walk by him. Suddenly, he was fully convinced that he had been carrying a dog this whole time. When he tried to picture seeing the goat at the fair for the first time, all he could see was a dog!

He shook his head, determined to end this nonsense once and for all. He began to put the goat down to check for himself what animal had been riding his shoulders for so long.

As soon as he had placed the animal down, robbers burst from behind the trees lining the path. They snatched what everyone could clearly see was a goat and ran off with it.

The man was left reeling and confused at what had just happened. After a few seconds, it all sank in and he realised how he had been fooled. He crouched down right there in the middle of the road and put his head in his hands.

He eventually made his way home empty-handed and told no one about his eventful walk home. It was a long time before he visited his aunt or cousins again.

11. A JACKAL AND THE FIGHTING GOATS

There once lived a cunning jackal who was always looking for an easy meal. He was not particularly intelligent but had become good at making other people work for him.

One day as he was out looking for food, he came upon two billy goats fighting on a hill. The goats were large, with big horns and strong hooves. They kept running towards each other and slamming their heads together. The jackal could tell that they had been going at this for a while. They were breathing heavily and their legs were trembling.

Ah, the jackal thought to himself. Here is the perfect opportunity. All I have to do is wait, and these goats will tire and wound themselves soon enough.

Settled at the base of the hill, the jackal watched the goats fight. They were mighty animals, determined and angry. The jackal watched as they slammed into each other so hard that their horns got caught. Agile and strong, neither was going to give up anytime soon. They twisted this way and that, dragging each other along until they were separated. Then they ran towards each other again.

Soon, the jackal noticed that the goats were getting tired. Their breath was heavier, the pauses between hits just a second

longer. This time when they rammed into each other, they drew blood.

The scent of the blood reached the jackal's nose, making his stomach rumble. He was getting hungrier and hungrier the longer he waited. He began to tremble with anticipation.

The goats were oblivious to the jackal watching and kept their eyes on each other. While they were beginning to get tired, they were nowhere near being exhausted enough to stop.

It was almost as though the hill was shaking from their rage. Who knew what they were so angry about? They themselves seemed to have forgotten. They had come here with their herd, which had left them behind after getting tired of the petty fight these two refused to settle. Now, it was simply a matter of pride.

Without noticing, both goats had drawn blood. It ran down their foreheads and onto the ground. The jackal could not resist anymore. Following his nose and his stomach, he began to lick the blood off the hill.

Now all the animals on the hill were unaware of one another, caught up in their heads. The goats were completely focused on their own pride, and the jackal was only thinking about getting all the blood into his belly.

The jackal followed the trail of blood up the hill, getting hungrier as he went up. He didn't notice how close he was to the goats and before anyone knew it, he was right in their path.

The goats charged at each other, oblivious to the jackal caught between them—he took the blow from both sides. All the breath rushed out of his lungs as he crashed onto the ground.

When the goats finally noticed him, they were spooked. How could they not have noticed a predator getting so close? They immediately turned and ran away.

The poor jackal could hardly breathe. He wheezed as he

tried to lift himself. His legs gave in, and he lay on the hill for a couple minutes while his heart returned to its normal rhythm. He realised that he was injured on both sides from the force of the goats' impact.

Bruised and bleeding the poor jackal finally dragged himself away to cower and lick his wounds. From that moment on, both him and the goats were more aware of themselves and their surroundings.

12. DHARMA

There once lived a man called Paapbuddhi who was always looking to cheat his way into making money. He was not particularly interested in working hard, or at all, and cared very little for things besides himself.

In the same village as him lived another man who could not be more different from him, named Dharmabuddhi. He was honest and fair in both his life and work.

Seeing Dharmabuddhi work, Paapbuddhi thought it would be easy to trick him and benefit from all his work. Dharma was a trusting man, and Paapbuddhi felt confident that he would be able to cheat a lot of money off him.

He approached Dharma with an offer to travel and work together. 'There are so many more opportunities out in the world. It will help us take care of our families and make sure they are comfortable for a long time. Plus, imagine all the stories we will have to tell!'

Though Dharmabuddhi was hesitant, he eventually agreed. The two men set off, travelling from village to town to city, picking up jobs wherever they were. Dharmabuddhi's work would always be done on time and be of the highest quality. People flocked around him naturally and were always sad when he had to leave.

Paapbuddhi had people charmed as well. His methods were very different from that of his travel companion. He often knew exactly what to say in any given situation, changing his personality and opinions from one conversation to the next. His work was sloppy and inadequate, though conveniently in ways that were only noticeable after he had left the place behind.

This went on for about three months before the two men decided they had earned enough to begin their journey back home. On the last day of their travels, Paapbuddhi stopped Dharmabuddhi to talk.

'Listen, we are travelling with an incredible amount of money and I don't want to risk it getting stolen. I just don't think it's safe,' he said.

'You're right,' Dharmabuddhi responded. 'It would be a shame if all our hard-earned money was lost so close to home.'

'Exactly my point. Here is what I think we should do. Right before we reach our village we should stop in the forest. We can bury our money safely there, taking a small sum between us. That way, we can return every time we need more, making sure no one but us knows where it is hidden.'

Dharmabuddhi was not used to doing things in this manner. Everything about him was transparent and upfront. But this was his first time being in possession of such a large amount of money, and he wanted to be responsible. So he agreed to Paapbuddhi's plan.

They found an old tree in the forest and buried the money deep within its roots. With just enough money to last them the month, they made their way back home.

A few weeks later, there was a knock on Dharmabuddhi's door. Opening it, he saw Paapbuddhi on the other side.

'Friend, I have come with a request. My portion of the

money has finished faster than I had thought, and I need to return to where we buried it. Will you be able to come with me tonight?' asked Paapbuddhi.

'Of course, of course,' Dharmabuddhi replied. 'You can join me and my family for dinner, and we can head out together.'

Later that night when the village was asleep, the two men made their way into the forest. They began to shovel in the moonlight, digging until they hit the box that held the money.

Dharmabuddhi got on his knees and reached into the hole they had dug, taking out the box. Brushing mud off its top, he opened it. While it was a full moon night, the shadows from the tress made it hard to see. It took his eyes a second to adjust, but when they did, he couldn't believe what was in front of him.

The box was empty! Dharmabuddhi looked into the pit, as if the money could have somehow slipped out of the box while it was buried. Behind him, Paapbuddhi had been quiet so far, but now spoke up.

'How could you? You stole it all!' he yelled.

Dharmabuddhi was shocked. 'Of course not! I haven't been back here since the time we buried it. Something else must have happened!'

'What else could it be? We were the only people who knew about this. You think you can cheat me out of my half so easily?' Paapbuddhi said furiously.

'I would never,' Dharmabuddhi tried to say, but Paapbuddhi was too upset to let him speak anymore.

'I can't trust you,' he said. 'The only way to resolve this is to take it to the panchayat. They will decide who is to blame for this.'

With that, Paapbuddhi stormed away with Dharmabuddhi running behind him, trying to explain that he had no idea how their money could have disappeared.

The next morning a panchayat was called. As Dharmabuddhi had never been accused of anything before, it drew a large crowd. No one could believe that he would do something like this, and no evidence of the money was found in his home either. In the end, it was decided that only the spirit of the tree by which the money was buried could give them an answer.

The panchayat was dispersed, ready to make their way to the tree spirit the next day. Paapbuddhi reached his home and took his father into a separate room to talk.

It was here that he finally confessed the truth. It was him who had gone and dug up all the money. He had wanted the money for himself and believed that if people could be convinced Dharmabuddhi had cheated him, the panchayat would offer him more money as compensation.

To make sure he wasn't found out, he needed his father's help. They needed to ensure that the tree spirit would tell everyone that it was Dharmabuddhi who had stolen the money.

'If you go and hide in the hollow of the tree before anyone else arrives,' Paapbuddhi said to his father, 'we can make sure everyone hears what we want them to believe.'

His father was easily tempted by the thought of having so much money to themselves and agreed to the plan.

When the panchayat made its way into the forest and towards the tree, both Dharmabuddhi and Paapbuddhi walked comfortably and with confidence. Upon reaching the tree, the village elder stepped forward.

This tree was old and wise and had watched many generations of humans come and go. Before it they placed their question, seeking the truth.

'O wise tree, please tell us what you saw. Thrice now the earth has been dug around your roots while you watched. We wish to know who it was that came and took everything the second time.'

From within the tree came a raspy voice, 'It was Dharmabuddhi. It was him who came alone and took all the money. He is the one who is guilty.'

Everyone was shocked. They had been sure of some other explanation, because the Dharmabuddhi they knew would never be capable of theft.

Dharmabuddhi was frowning. He knew that it wasn't him who had stolen the money, so how could the tree have seen him? Knowing that there was some kind of trickery going on, he took matters into his own hands.

Before anyone could stop him, he had gathered dry leaves and sticks laying on the forest floor and placed them near the tree. He then set them on fire. People watched in horror as smoke rose and entered the tree, convinced that this was his way of getting petty revenge.

The smoke quickly entered the hollow of the tree, causing Paapbuddhi's father inside to choke. He began to cough and wheeze, as his son ran to save him from the fire.

As soon as Paapbuddhi got his breathless father out of the tree, they knew there was nothing else they could do. With his hands together, the father confessed everything.

Paapbuddhi was firmly punished by the panchayat and lived the rest of his life in shame. All they money was found in his home and given to Dharmabuddhi, who lived a comfortable life, working with people he trusted.

13. THE TIGER WHO WAS A DONKEY

There once lived a donkey who belonged to a washerman. The washerman was a good and hard worker, though he was not so good with his money. It was not that he did not have enough of it—it was that when he did have it, he found it hard to let go. He would refuse to spend it on things that were necessary, even on if they would make his life easier.

Whenever he needed something, he always looked for some kind of alternative or jugaad first. Due to this habit his life was often harder than it needed to be, but the one that ended up facing the worst consequences was his donkey.

The washerman and his donkey would go from house to house collecting people's laundry. The donkey would wait patiently by the gate as his owner counted the clothes and let people know exactly how much they would owe him. While some people were annoyed by this, most appreciated his consistency and honesty.

After the collection process was over, they made their way to the river to get started on the washing. The donkey's real hard work began after the clothes had all been washed. Heavy from the water, the clothes were piled on his back to be carried back to their home. There, the man would carefully hang them

all up to dry. The walk was not particularly long, but as time went by it became harder and harder for the donkey.

The washerman had begun to take on more work but failed to take care of his donkey accordingly. The grass around their house was dry and brown, not providing enough fuel for the donkey to keep working the way he was. The washerman did not have the time to take his donkey to greener pastures and refused to buy food for him to eat.

As time went on, the donkey became frail, walking slowly and stumbling often. The washerman was worried and just about to give in and buy some straw for the donkey to eat when he stumbled upon an idea.

While taking a stroll near the forest, his eye caught on something. Walking a little into the forest he saw that it was a tiger, one that seemed to have died recently. This gave him an idea that caused the donkey a great deal of misery.

He skinned the tiger and took home its skin. There, he carefully moulded it around the donkey's body. This way, if someone was far away, they would think that it was a real tiger.

This disguise meant that the donkey could now go graze safely in places without the washerman. He would remain safe from wild animal attacks and farmers chasing him off their property.

The next few days brought about a new routine in their lives. Every evening, the man would dress his donkey in the tiger skin and send him out to graze. In the fading light of the setting sun, the donkey's disguise worked especially well.

One night, the donkey was out in a field while the neighbours puzzled over why a tiger would be wandering in the vegetable patch. They were too scared to check, so the donkey continued his munching. It was a pleasant evening with a cool breeze and the donkey felt good. Strength had begun to return to his body.

The quiet of the night was suddenly broken by the braying of another donkey in the distance. The tiger-skin donkey looked up, his ears flicking. Soon enough there was another bray and he answered back. His voice was loud and echoed into the night.

By now, people had come out of their houses to see where this noisy donkey was braying from. They'd all had a long day of working in the sun and did not appreciate their peace being broken by such an annoying animal.

Standing outside, they realised the noise was coming from what they had thought was a tiger this whole time! On checking closely, it was very obviously a donkey. They could see him now, lifting his long neck towards the sky and braying.

Realising that they had been fooled, their rage only grew. Picking up their laathis they began to chase the donkey off their property. Where once they would have only used the laathis to threaten, this time they were angry enough to get in a few good hits before the donkey ran off.

Bruised and aching, the donkey returned home to the washerman. He was horrified to see what had become of his poor animal. Hearing people talk the next day, he discovered what must have happened. Shamefaced, he kept quiet and bought some good straw and hay for his donkey before going home.

14. THE FOX'S CAVE

In an old cave located deep in the jungle lived a fox. He had found it many summers ago and it had kept him warm and safe ever since. Not many animals knew of it, as it lay beyond the river, behind a curtain of vines.

The cave soon became an incredibly safe place for the fox. He would go there to recover after long days or whenever the outside world became too much for him. There was a cozy spot in one of its corners where some soft grass grew. The fox would curl up here at night. Right above it, the cave's ceiling had a small crack that let the sun in during the day and let him stargaze at night. It was the fox's favourite place.

One day, the fox was out hunting and eating with his friends when a tiger chanced upon the cave. The tiger was new to this jungle and was spending his first few weeks exploring the area. He had found great corners from where he could crouch and pounce on his prey. This jungle seemed to be full of potential.

Upon seeing the cave he got even more excited. Even though it was fairly hidden, he could see a great number of footsteps leading to and from it. Hmm, he thought to himself, this seems to be a place someone visits frequently. Whoever they are, they are sure to return soon. If I wait hidden inside, my meal shall walk right to me.

So, the tiger entered the cave and settled down to wait with great anticipation.

As the sun began to set, the fox made his way back to his cave. It was a busy day with his friends that had ended with his belly full and his heart content. He hummed a little tune as he walked but suddenly stopped when he reached the mouth of the cave.

Being a detail-oriented animal, something felt off to him. Heavy footsteps—that he could tell belonged to a tiger—were leading into the cave. He began to back up but then paused. What if the tiger had left? There was a smaller opening at the back of the cave from where he could squeeze in.

Not wanting to be scared until he had evidence that there was something to be scared of, the fox began to think. He did not want to take the risk of actually going into the cave to check, so he came up with a different plan.

The fox walked up to the cave, took a deep breath and said, 'Hello cave! It is so good to see you after the long day I've had. May I come in?'

There was only silence in response. The fox tried again.

'Cave, how come you are so silent today? Usually you greet me so lovingly. Have I upset you?'

Again there was no response from the cave.

'I can see you are upset about something. It's alright, I shall spend the night somewhere else today.'

Inside the cave the tiger was confused. He had never heard of a talking cave before. But he was new to this jungle. Perhaps it was common here to have caves that greet you before you entered them. If that were true, the cave must be silent and

angry because he had entered it without any greeting. Not wanting the fox to leave, the tiger cried out.

'Please enter, dear animal! I am so happy to see you!'

The tiger's voice was fierce and loud. It was made even scarier by the echo caused by the cave's walls. Hearing it made the fox's hair stand on end and confirmed his great fear.

The fox turned and ran away as fast as he could. He spent the next few nights with family and friends, protected by their company. It was a long time before he approached another cave.

As for the tiger, he learned that the animals in this jungle were far cleverer than him and thought well before he blindly believed in something again.

15. MANAV, PRANAV, GAURAV AND SAHIL

There were once four friends, Manav, Pranav, Gaurav and Sahil, who had known each other for a long time. Growing up together they had spent many days discussing their dreams and futures. Even as life took them in different directions, they always had each other to rely on.

Manav, Pranav and Gaurav decided to go out in search of glory and sacred knowledge. They wanted to know as much about the world as they could—where things came from, where they went and if they could be brought back.

Sahil decided to stay on in his little town and live a simple life. He was not a very curious person and was happy with what he had. Over the years, even as his friends loved him, they began to look down on him for not seeking knowledge the way they did.

One summer after not having seen each other for a few months, they all met up again. They sat down for an afternoon chai and began to catch up on what each of them had been up to. Soon, Sahil found himself excluded from the conversation as the rest of them talked about everything they had learned—how they had all found different sages and gurus to guide them. Every time he tried to tell them something about himself, he

was brushed off.

Quietly sipping his chai, Sahil listened to his friends talk. They had all changed so much, he thought to himself. So many of these things they have learned are things I had never even considered, thinking them impossible.

As the day went on, Manav, Gaurav and Pranav began to get restless. It was all well and good to talk about things they knew, but they wanted to go out and see what all they could do with it. They began to make plans. Chatting among themselves, they decided to go out and look for opportunities to put their newfound knowledge to test.

They were just getting up from the table when they remembered Sahil. Glancing at him, they felt bad. While they did think that he was wasting his life, perhaps leaving him behind would be too harsh. Maybe the journey would inspire him as well! With that thought, they invited him to come along.

Sahil was not very interested in joining them. All afternoon he had been ignored and brushed aside. But these were his childhood friends! For old times' sake, he accepted their offer and came along.

Walking through the forest at the edge of the town, the friends chanced upon the body of a lion that had recently passed away. Manav, Pranav and Gaurav got excited and exchanged knowing looks. Sahil was just confused. What could they possibly plan to do with a dead lion?

'What am I missing?' he asked. 'What is so exciting about this lion?'

Manav grinned. 'We are going to bring it back to life, of course!'

'It will be truly glorious, just wait and watch,' Pranav added.

'The most impressive thing you will have ever seen!'

Gaurav said.

'I really don't think that's a good idea at all. What are you planning to do once he is alive? Don't you think his first thought will be to kill us all?' Sahil said, worried.

'That is just a sign of how little you know. The lion will be too grateful to us for bringing him back to life to even consider killing us,' Manav said wisely.

'I'm not so sure. A lion's instincts are not so easily changed,' Sahil insisted.

His friends were now getting annoyed.

'That just shows how little you know. You were not out there for months learning all that there is to know about the world! Let us do what we know best,' Pranav snapped.

Sahil twisted his hands together, unsure still. He knew his friends had stopped taking him seriously. But he didn't want to die because of their foolish actions.

'Wait for me to climb this tree before you begin,' he said. 'I fear my nervousness will just distract you. It will be better if I get out of your way.'

Sahil found the tallest tree nearby and climbed it as high as he could. He found a thick branch that could hold his weight and settled on it. It gave him a good view of everything his friends were doing on the ground.

Next to the lion his friends were beginning to go through the steps to bring the animal back to life. He watched them chant and run around, waving their arms in the air. They walked around the lion three times and then stood still.

It felt as though the whole world was holding its breath—waiting. After what felt like hours but was actually just a few seconds, they watched the lion begin to stir.

Sahil couldn't help but let out a small gasp. There was a part of him that had not fully believed what his friends were attempting was possible. But the proof of their abilities was visible to him now.

They all watched the lion's chest begin to rise and fall as the breath returned to his body. He lifted his head and blinked slowly, taking in the world around him.

Manav, Pranav and Gaurav were frozen next to the lion. It became apparent to Sahil from the looks on their faces that they had never done anything like this before either. Perhaps a part of them had not expected to get this far.

By now, the lion seemed to have become fully aware of himself and his surroundings. The second his eyes landed on the three men standing beside him, his whole body went stiff. Before Sahil could even blink, the lion took a mighty leap towards his friends on the ground. There wasn't even time for anyone to scream before the lion's claws were ripping into them.

Sahil remained clinging to the tree as his friends screams reached his ears. He hadn't even realised when he closed his eyes and tucked his face behind the tree trunk. By the time he felt brave enough to open his eyes again, the lion was long gone.

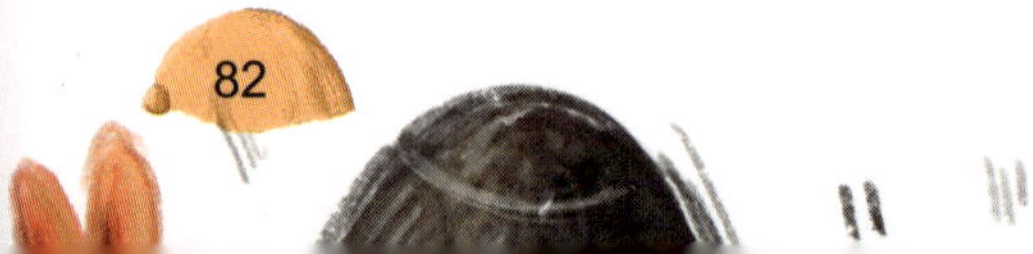

16. BED BUGS, THE MOSQUITO AND THE KING

This is the story of a family of bed bugs who once lived in the fanciest house. There were perhaps no other insects who lived in such luxury. Every night they were treated to a feast, delivered to them without fail. All they had to do was lie in bed and wait—for this little bed bug family happened to live in the palace of a king to a rich kingdom. They had lived a humble life once, living with a mattress-maker in the village. Then one day their whole life had turned upside down. Barely hanging on, they had been attached to a mattress that was carried carefully to be delivered personally to the king.

When everything had finally stopped swaying, the family had emerged tentatively out of hiding. They looked around in awe at their new surroundings—the carved bedframe their mattress now sat upon and the embroidered sheets covering it. There were heavy pillows all along one side of the bed with hand fans laid next to them.

They looked at each other in disbelief. They knew immediately they must be in the palace. They had heard the mattress-maker talk about it, the glory of having been asked to make something directly for the king.

Every night from then on, they would wait for the king to

retire to his room. Once he had got into bed, they all stayed very still until they knew he was in a deep sleep. Only then would they bite him, always near his feet to make sure they were not discovered.

They lived this way for many months. Soon, they could barely remember what their lives had been like before. It felt like some sort of a miracle to have ended up in a place like this.

One day they were visited by a mosquito. She was a daredevil, a risktaker. She was rarely in one place for very long as she often had to fly away from annoyed humans trying to swat and squash her. This was not her first time in the palace. She had often wandered its halls, crashing banquets and exploring the servants quarters. Today, she chanced upon the king's room.

Catching sight of her, the bed bugs came out to say hi.

'Hello! What brings you here today?' one bug asked.

The mosquito was distracted, flitting about from one side of the room to the other. Glancing at the bugs on the bed, she nodded a quick greeting before returning to her inspection.

The bugs watched her buzz about the room, going from corner to corner, occasionally disappearing behind something or the other.

'Are you looking for something?' they finally asked.

'Oh no!' the mosquito replied, finally slowing down and approaching the bed. 'I'm sorry I've been so rude! It's just that I've never been to this room before.'

'It's the king's room!' boasted one of the little bugs.

This caught the mosquito's attention. 'Really? I thought it must be someone important because of how fancy the room is, but for it to belong to the king himself...'

The bed bugs had never had anything to show off before. They got excited when they saw how in awe of everything the mosquito was. One of them told her very excitedly, 'The room's not even the best part! Every night we get to feast on the king himself.'

The mosquito looked like her eyes might pop out of her head. 'Are you telling the truth? I don't believe you!'

'It's true, it's true!' the bed bugs said. 'It's unlike anything you've ever tried!'

The mosquito had a glint in her eye. 'I've always wanted to try royal blood. I've seen the type of food they make for him. Anyone who eats like that regularly must be truly delicious.'

She looked at the bed bugs, how happy and content they seemed. Settling on the bed beside them, she made her request.

'Oh, please let me join your feast tonight. It would be a dream come true if you allowed me.'

The bed bugs all looked at each other, unsure whether to allow this request. Finally, an older bed bug said, 'We have been so careful about when and where to bite. How can we be sure that you will not get us discovered?'

'I promise to be just as careful. I shall follow your every rule if you will only let me get a taste of the king's blood.'

'You must make sure to bite him only after you are sure that he is fast asleep. Otherwise he will wake up and discover us all. Try not to bite close to his face as he is most likely to feel that immediately. Can you follow these rules?' the older bug said.

'Yes, yes, I can follow them.'

'Okay, then you may join us tonight.'

When night fell, the bed bugs disappeared within the bed to wait for the king. The mosquito sat on top of the bedframe, quivering with excitement. She saw the king come in, get ready for bed and then lie down. She flew above his face and watched as his breathing began to slow. She couldn't stop herself anymore.

She knew she must only bite him near his feet, but the thought of that fresh blood near his face, so close to his heart, tempted her. She settled on his nose and bit down.

The king immediately woke up. He swatted at his face, annoyed at the buzzing in his ears. Out of the corner of his eye he saw the mosquito fly away. He began to scream for his guards, yelling about how the king's room had not been cleaned properly.

Guards and servants rushed in, opening windows and stripping the sheets off the bed. At the king's insistence the entire room got a deep clean. The bed bugs tried to escape but were caught. Some were killed and some thrown out, leaving them to scatter and find shelter, cursing the stupid mosquito. She had managed to ruin their whole life in her moment of greed.

This was the tragic and sudden end to their life of comfort and indulgence.

17. GOLD COINS AND PRACTICAL DAUGHTERS

There was once a humble farmer who worked tirelessly on his field day and night. He was a wheat farmer and having a very hard year. Despite his hard labour, due to a dry spell during the monsoon, he had not been able to grow much.

On a particularly difficult day, he went to sit by a tree in the shade to get a break from the heat. He sat heavily on the ground with his back against the tree trunk and let out a deep sigh, closing his eyes. His spirits were low, as he worried about how he would feed his family this year.

A few moments later, the farmer opened his eyes and began to get up. Just as he was beginning to rise, he noticed something out of the corner of his eye and froze. There, emerging from near an anthill, was a mighty cobra. It was a truly majestic creature, holding itself up with pride.

The farmer had deep respect for nature. He believed the cobra to be a patron of the land and his field and bowed to him respectfully. He then went inside to fetch the cobra a bowl of cool water, since it was such a hot day. He placed it gently near the cobra and then returned to his work.

The next day, when he went to retrieve his bowl, he saw something marvelous. Inside the bowl lay a shiny gold coin. The

farmer picked up the coin, not believing his eyes. He accepted this blessing with deep gratitude and was able to feed his family a warm and hearty meal after many days.

From that day on the farmer began to leave a bowl of water for the snake every day. The next morning, without fail, he would find a gold coin within the bowl.

This changed the fate of the farmer and his family. What had started as a difficult and harsh season turned into one of abundance. Their nights turned from worrying about their next meal to ones of laughter and joy.

A month later, the farmer was leaving to visit his sister who lived in another village. Before leaving, he gave careful instructions to his daughter to bring the cobra water every day when he was gone. His daughter was a smart and practical girl and promised to do as he said.

She went to the field the morning after her father had left and placed the bowl of water for the cobra by the tree. The next day she was shocked to see a gold coin in the bowl! She thought to herself, this cobra must have found treasure somewhere nearby. Where else was he getting gold coins from? Surely if she could capture him she would be able to find it. Then her family would be rich and have to depend on no one. With this in mind, she came back the next morning—not with a bowl of water, but with a stick.

She attacked the snake, who hissed in pain. Before she could get another hit in, the snake bit her ankle, poisoning her.

She passed away soon after and the entire village mourned her loss. The farmer rushed home after hearing the news and was devastated. There were many people who were angry and tried to convince him to take revenge on the snake.

'How can you simply let this go? She was your child and must be avenged!'

No matter what anyone said, the farmer was not convinced. While a part of him understood the cobra's actions, the bigger reason for his not killing the snake was that he had begun to rely heavily on it. So, he went out to his field with a bowl of water and left it where he usually did for the cobra to find.

The next day, however, instead of a gold coin, the farmer found the cobra itself waiting for him.

'We cannot continue this way anymore,' the snake told the farmer.

'What do you mean? I have brought you water like always,' the farmer said.

'How can you say that? Your child has passed, and all you care for is your gold coin. What started as a sign of respect has turned into simple greed. Instead of mourning your daughter you are here, dishonouring her memory.'

The farmer slowly turned red with shame and was not able to say anything.

'Here,' the cobra said, placing a diamond on the ground. 'Keep this as a final token from me. We will not be seeing each other from this day on.'

With that, the cobra slithered away, leaving the farmer in his empty field. As the farmer stood all by himself in the field that used to be his pride and joy, everything seemed to hit him at once. The grief of his daughter's passing seemed to sink in for what felt like the first time. He picked up the diamond and began walking home, tears running down his face.

18. THE JACKAL AND THE SINGING DONKEY

There once was a donkey who lived with a washerman. They worked together during the day, with the donkey carrying the load of clothes on his back. At night, the washerman would let the donkey roam free to graze in the nearby grass fields.

The donkey soon grew tired of the taste of grass and longed for something new. Something fresh and juicy. His gaze began to linger on the vegetable patch of a nearby farm. After a few nights of longing, he couldn't resist anymore. One night, instead of staying in his field, he broke through the farm's fence and munched on the fresh brinjal growing there.

A few nights later the donkey was spotted by a jackal. The jackal would often hunt farm animals at night, and the donkey and him began to run into each other regularly. They were soon friends, chatting about their days as they ate.

One night, the donkey was in an exceptionally good mood. The moon was full, giving everything a soft blue glow. The donkey, who was bigger and stronger now, broke the fence of the farm and grinned. The jackal followed behind carefully and looked up at the donkey.

'How come you are so happy tonight?' he asked.

'How could I not be? I have the promise of good food

before me, a friend by my side and the moon is so beautiful tonight! It makes me want to burst into song!'

'Please don't,' the jackal said. 'We will surely get caught if you do.'

'What are you talking about? I have an incredibly soft voice, you know,' replied the donkey.

Hearing this the jackal gave him a funny look. 'Who told you that? Because I must tell you, whoever it was, lied to you.'

'No one had to tell me,' the donkey said indignantly. 'I can hear myself perfectly well, and a night like this deserves to have someone sing about it.'

The jackal could see that the silly donkey had made up his mind. Not wanting to get caught up in whatever mess the donkey was going to create, he made his request, 'Okay, if you must sing, please wait till I have crossed the farm gate. Then you can sing to your heart's desire.'

The donkey, while confused, accepted these terms and watched the jackal scurry away. When he was a safe distance away, the donkey could resist it no longer.

He began to sing with great enthusiasm. With his head swaying, he really looked like he was singing something beautiful. Unfortunately, that was not the case. His voice was hoarse and out of tune as he continued to bray into the quiet night.

Soon enough what the jackal had feared came true. Hearing the donkey bray so loudly woke the farmers, who rushed out to see what was causing such a commotion so late at night. Upon seeing the donkey in the middle of their vegetable patch, they started towards him with heavy laathis.

The poor donkey was so caught up in what he thought was a beautiful song that he saw them too late. He began to run, but the farmers were able to get a few strong hits in with their

laathis. They chased him off their farm, the laathis whacking and swinging behind him. The jackal watched from where he lay hidden, wincing in sympathy.

Once the farmers had all gone back to their homes, the jackal went up to the now-limping donkey.

'How badly did they hit you?' the jackal asked.

'What do you think? They got some strong hits in, I'm bruised for sure,' the grumpy donkey answered.

'I did try to warn you. Hopefully you will now think twice about where you choose to have your next concert,' said the cheeky jackal.

'Hmph! It's not my fault that no one here knows how to appreciate good music!'

The jackal laughed. He did notice, however, that the next time they met up, the donkey was extra careful to be quiet.

19. THE TURTLE AND THE DOVES

This is the story of an unlikely trio of friends—two doves and a turtle. The doves often stopped by the pond near the turtle's home, and he became curious about their travels. Soon, they were best friends. The turtle had never ventured far from the pond and loved hearing about the world through the doves' stories.

As winter approached, the doves had to migrate, but for the first time, they weren't as excited. They saw the turtle's sadness and knowing their time together was short one dove said, 'Turtle, we don't want to leave you—it's just that we can't take you with us.'

'I never realised how big the world was until I met you,' the turtle replied. The doves wished he could come and knew they couldn't just leave him behind.

In the week before their departure, the friends spent as much time together as possible, but the turtle grew sadder each day. Finally, the doves came up with a plan.

'Do you think you could come with us?' they asked. 'We'll be very careful.'

'Really?' the turtle exclaimed.

'We'll carry a stick between us and you'll hold on. But you

must be careful—if you fall, we don't know if we can save you.'

'I promise,' said the eager turtle.

The next morning, they began their journey, picking a sturdy branch for the turtle to hold with his mouth. The doves flew slowly, making sure the branch stayed steady. From the sky, everything seemed small to the turtle—his world was so much bigger than he had realised.

They passed the forest the turtle had lived in and then flew above a village. The turtle watched the people below with interest. But were pointing and laughing at him?

Annoyed and insulted, the turtle opened his mouth to ask, 'What are you looking at?'

But before he could say more, he lost his grip. The doves tried desperately to catch him, but the turtle fell. Tragically, he crashed to the ground, his adventure ending before it even began.

20. PIGEONS WORKING TOGETHER

One hot summer afternoon, a flock of pigeons were flying across a clear sky. They had been together for many seasons and knew each other well. They were led by a strong and smart leader who they followed happily and with pride.

They were out looking for food, flying above fields, huts and little clusters of trees. They knew this area well and kept a keen eye on the ground.

As they were flying they spotted something unusual. In a large clearing, someone had tossed a bunch of seeds. It was enough to feed them all and more. Seeing this, the flock got very excited. How lucky they were to have spotted it before any other bird!

'Looks like we shall be eating well today!' a pigeon said as they began to descend.

'Yes! Oh, I can already feel how full I'm going to be,' another pigeon said eagerly.

They all happily cooed amongst themselves, not noticing that their leader had been silent so far. She wanted to be excited about this find as well, but she did not trust it. She had been leading her flock for a long time and knew this area well. It did not make sense to her to one day simply find food like this,

ready for them to eat. She could find no reason for it not to be a trap.

'I think we should keep going and eat somewhere else today,' she said, turning towards the rest of the pigeons.

'Why would we do that? There's more than enough here,' another pigeon replied.

'I think it's a trap. Why else would someone leave seeds laid out like this?' she said.

'You can't really think that! Besides, I can't see a trap anywhere.'

'Just because we cannot see it doesn't mean it can't be there! Humans have always been cunning, I'm sure they are the ones behind this,' she replied.

The rest of the pigeons looked at each other. Perhaps they could have been convinced if they hadn't already become excited about this field filled with food. Their leader looked at them and knew they didn't want to listen to her. She sighed.

'Alright. Go ahead if you wish, but I will not be joining you.' With that, she went and perched on a tree at the edge of the field.

The rest of the flock squawked with delight and went straight for the seeds. They all settled down on the ground and began to eat as their leader watched on.

It turns out that the leader was right to be suspicious. After a little while, the pigeons realised they could not move from the spot they had landed. Their feet were completely stuck in a net that had been laid by a bird-catcher, hidden beneath the seeds and grass.

The birds began to panic, flapping their wings as hard as they could. However, it was hopeless. They were stuck quite firmly to the net and were not going anywhere.

Their leader flew down from her branch and hovered

above them. She knew they did not have a lot of time and that the bird-catcher would soon be on his way back. She needed to figure out a way to help her flock—and fast!

'I need everyone to calm down!' she cried, 'Don't waste your energy on something that isn't going to work.'

She looked hard at the net and all the birds stuck to it, and a plan began to form in her mind.

'Okay, I know what we have to do. We aren't going to be able to get rid of the net, but it doesn't look too heavy. If you all work together you can lift it up into the air with you.'

'I—I'm not so sure,' a pigeon replied nervously.

The rest of the flock looked at each other, all of them unsure. Lifting the entire net into the sky? It seemed hopeless.

'Trust me! How long have we been flying together? You know each other well and have all taken care of each other at some point or another. I know you can do this,' she responded confidently.

Hearing this gave the flock some hope. They knew how to work together and trusted their leader to guide them. They looked at her and nodded.

'Okay, I'll count you all down,' she said. 'Everyone needs to start flapping their wings on three, got it?'

'Got it!' came the cry from the pigeons.

'One, two ... three!'

The birds began to flap their wings all together, getting faster and faster. Slowly, they noticed they were beginning to rise! They kept going and were soon in the air—the net, still heavy with seeds, dangling from their feet.

'Follow me,' their leader instructed. 'I know who can help.'

So the birds flew behind her, carrying the net with them. She led them to a place where two little mice lived. She explained all that had happened, and the mice were more than happy to help.

They scurried between the pigeons, biting through the net with their sharp teeth. Soon all the pigeons were free, shaking their claws free from the torn net.

'Thank you so much,' the leader pigeon said to the mice.

'Of course! We animals have to look out for each other when we can,' the mice replied. 'It was quite impressive how you all carried the net here too.'

'Ah, that was her idea,' a pigeon said proudly, gesturing towards their leader.

Now that they were all free from the net, the mice and the pigeons all sat together and munched on the seeds that had been carried over. They laughed and talked well into the night, happy to be with each other.

21. THE JACKAL AND THE DRUM

In a dense forest lived a young jackal, his hunger growing each day. Every morning, he'd set off to find enough food to grow strong. He had always been anxious, which made him cautious and aware of his surroundings.

One day, while searching for food, he stumbled upon a battlefield littered with broken carts, weapons and armour, torn flags and debris. Among the wreckage, he spotted a huge drum leaning against a tree.

The jackal carefully navigated the mess, looking for food. Suddenly, a chilling noise pierced the air—BOOM! It was loud and unlike anything he had ever heard, sending a jolt of fear through him. Terrified, he ran back into the forest, where he knew what each sound was, what was safe and what wasn't.

After putting some distance between himself and the source of the noise, the jackal paused to catch his breath. As his fear faded, curiosity took over. He decided to return and find out what had caused the noise.

The jackal walked back to the battlefield, where the sound echoed again. It frightened him, but he noticed it didn't seem to get any closer.

When he reached the field again, he was annoyed. The sound was still booming, but it seemed harmless. He followed it to the tree where the drum stood. There, the cause of the noise became clear—the wind was making the branches hit the drum, creating the booming sound that had scared the jackal so badly.

Relieved, the jackal resumed his search for food and soon found plenty to eat. As a gentle breeze blew by, the branches hit the drum again, but this time, the jackal only flinched slightly.

22. THE CRAB AND THE CRANE

There was once a wide and deep lake that was home to many creatures. They spent sunny days lounging on rocks, hunting fish and sharing gossip.

One of these creatures was an aging crane. He had lived by the lake his whole life, depending on it for food. He was also the one who brought news of the outside world. He would fly all over and bring back stories to tell everyone who couldn't leave the lake.

However, as the years went by, it became harder to hunt. His senses were not as sharp, his body not as fast. He grew worried about how he would continue to feed himself.

Slowly, he came up with a cunning plan. It was a clever one indeed, where the food would come to him instead of him having to chase after it.

One day, he sat by the lake and began to cry. His soft weeping alerted the animals who became concerned. A crab swam towards him and asked, 'What's the matter, Crane? Why are you sitting here crying instead of finding fish to eat?'

'Oh, dear Crab,' the crane sighed, 'What is the point of eating anymore? I have just heard the most tragic news.'

'What is it? What has happened?' the crab was now quite worried.

'The humans are saying that there will be no rain this year and our lake will lose too much water.'

'What does that mean?' the crab asked. A crowd of animals had gathered, anxious to know more.

'The lake will dry up,' the crane replied sadly. 'I fear most of us will not make it.'

This caused panic among the animals. How could the lake that had kept them safe for years dry up? Would they just wait for this tragedy to occur?

In the chaos, the crab cried out, 'There must be something we can do!'

The crane sniffled and said, 'Perhaps I can help. There's a lake not far from here with enough water to hold us all through the dry season. I could carry you all there.'

'Would you truly do that for us, Crane?'

'Of course! But there's one condition. My wings aren't as strong, so I can only carry one at a time.'

The crab looked at the fish. 'That should be fine. If you begin now, we'll be relocated in time.'

'Don't worry,' the crane cried, 'You can all rely on me! Let me take a fish there now.'

The crane scooped a fish into his beak and flew away. As he flew east, the fish, peeking out, saw no lake. The crane's plan was working. He had overheard no human conversation; there was enough water for everyone!

The crane landed on a rock far from the lake and ate the fish he'd promised to relocate. He returned, telling everyone how happy the fish was in the new lake.

For many days, this continued. The crane would take a fish, eat it and return.

The crab had watched the crane fly the fish away for about a week before he got impatient. He, too, wanted to see this new lake. So, he went to the crane and made his request.

'Crane, won't you take me to the new lake?'

'Of course,' replied the crane, who was growing tired of only eating fish. 'Tell you what, I'll take you on the next trip.'

'Really? You've done so much for us,' the crab said. 'Without you, we wouldn't even know our lake was in danger!'

'Oh, it's nothing,' the crane said, waving his wing. 'It's what anyone would do.'

The crab climbed onto the crane's back. They flew through the clouds, away from the lake. The crab looked down but saw only trees, fields and huts.

'Crane, where's the lake?' the crab asked.

'It's up ahead. Don't worry, it's hard to spot,' the crane replied.

The crane, proud of his trick, couldn't resist bragging. 'There's no new lake,' he confessed, 'I just wanted an easy meal.'

The crab listened, horrified to discover there was no new lake. He looked down and noticed a rock with a heap of fish bones scattered on top. Furious, he squeezed the crane's neck with his sharp claws until it lay limp on the rock instead of him.

When the crab returned, all the creatures were surprised. 'Why are you back?' they asked. 'Where's the crane?'

Just as the crab began to explain how they'd been tricked, it began to rain, filling the lake anew.

23. THE THREE FISH

There once lay a little river by a village. It was not particularly large or impressive, but it was home to many happy and fulfilled fish. They would swim from one end of the riverbank to the other, their days warm and content.

Among the school of fish were three fish, who were the best of friends. They spent all their time together. They would eat, sunbathe, lazily swim around and watch the tadpoles turn into frogs.

Their personalities balanced each other well. Lal was quieter, happy to go along with what the others were doing. Shweta and Sona often came to him and whenever they needed quiet comfort or some advice. Apart from being wise, he was also secretly funny—something people only discovered after getting to know him well.

Shweta was the planner among them. If they ever got into trouble, it was usually Shweta behind it. She was sharp, clever and easily bored. She was always looking for ways to make her friends laugh and coming up with new games to play.

Sona was the stubborn one. She decided which part of the river they were going to or which games they would play that day. She was protective about what was hers and refused to let anything go. All the bullies mostly left the three of them alone because she once yelled at them so aggressively that they had cried. No one had taken the bullies seriously since.

One morning, Lal was hanging out in the cool shade of a lily pad when he overheard something. He liked to have some quiet time to himself in the mornings, and this was turning into a morning unlike any other. On the surface were two fishermen, talking about their fishing plans for tomorrow.

Lal knew immediately that he had to warn his friends. They needed to be able to protect themselves and make sure they could all stay together! He swam as fast as he could to the place they met at each morning. Shweta and Sona were already there waiting for him. They stared at him in alarm as he sped towards them.

'Ha–hee—' he wheezed, unable to get any words out.

'What are you in such a rush for? Is someone chasing you? I swear I've made them cry once, and I am not scared to do it again,' Sona said, ready to fight.

'Let him catch his breath before you start throwing threats around, Sona! Lal, what has happened?'

Lal took a deep breath before telling them all that he had heard—how the fishermen were coming with their nets and would be capturing a bunch of fish tomorrow.

'We need to be on guard. We have to stick together and make sure to be safe,' he said.

Shweta and Sona were stunned. They could not imagine their home, which had been a safe haven for them for so long, was under threat. After they had digested the news a little, Shweta finally spoke.

'Okay. If we remain alert and aware we should all be fine. We are small enough that if we don't panic we can wiggle out of the net even if we do get caught. Right?' she said, looking to her

friends for reassurance.

Lal nodded. 'We know this river well. We can make sure to stay somewhere the fishermen's net won't reach us.'

They both turned to look towards Sona. She had been strangely silent up till then. Looking at her now, they could see her beginning to get angry.

'How dare those fishermen think they can scare us like this? We will not be made to run around and hide in our own home!' she exclaimed.

'Sona, this is not something you can fight by yourself like this,' Lal tried to explain. 'Those humans are clever and have all kinds of tricks we cannot understand. The best thing we can do is to protect ourselves.'

'No, no! I refuse to be scared like this! They can do their best but they won't be able to capture me,' Sona said stubbornly.

Shweta and Lal looked at each other despairingly. They knew there was very little point in trying to argue with Sona when she had made up her mind about something. But this was different. If she wasn't careful it would end up costing her life.

Amreen tried to reason with her, 'Sona, please. This is not like anything we have ever faced before. Don't be hardheaded about this.'

No matter how much they tried, Sona would not budge. She was convinced she could treat this problem the way she had treated every other that had come her way—by throwing herself against it until it went away.

The next day the fishermen were on their boats, ready with their nets. It was a clear day, good for fishing.

When they reached the middle of the river, they began to lower the net. It disappeared under the water, sinking deeper and deeper. By now, Lal had safely tucked himself away near the riverbed. Between the pebbles and moss, he knew he was protected. He was worried about his friends—Sona especially.

Shweta had been anxiously swimming around, going from one spot to the other, unable to settle. When she saw the net appear in the water she swam as fast as she could in the opposite direction. When her fin got caught in the net, she breathed through the panic. She twisted herself slowly and was able to free herself.

Sona was the only one who refused to be cautious. She did not hide or try to run when the net got too close. She soon found herself caught and tangled, unable to escape.

When the waters were finally calm, Lal and Shweta emerged from their hiding spots to look for each other. When they saw each other and found that neither of them knew where Saida was, they knew immediately what must have happened.

They were heartbroken and mourned their friend together, forever remembering her and the warm days they spent together.

24. THE HARE AND THE LION

In a big, dense forest lived an arrogant lion. He was the strongest creature among all the animals who lived here and he knew it. Not a day went by when he was not attacking the other animals, eating all that his heart desired.

The rest of the animals spent most of their days in constant fear because of the lion. They could never relax or have fun because they were always worried about who he would attack next. They were exhausted and dreamed of feeling safe in their forest once more.

Finally, they decided they had had enough. If things kept going the way they were, soon there would be no animals left in the forest at all. All the animals gathered together to come up with a plan. Some of the physically stronger animals thought that everyone should band together to challenge the lion to a fight. They were very quickly reminded by the others of the lion's strength and how nothing was a match for it. The deer tried to think of ways to drive the lion out of the forest, while the elephants wondered if they could perhaps crush him.

'It's completely hopeless!' cried a bear, 'There's no way we will be able to get rid of him. We should instead start looking for somewhere else to live ourselves.'

'Don't be ridiculous!' said a brave little hare. 'This is my home and nothing can drive me away! I was here before this lion arrived, and I shall stay here till he is gone. There must be a way we can fool him somehow.'

'What do you have in mind, Hare? Do you really think we could be free of the lion?' the bear said tentatively.

'You have been blinded by his strength, Bear. Just because someone is strong does not always mean that they are smart as well. The lion has relied on his strength to get him everything in life, never once using his brain. I'm sure if we stop fearing him, we will be able to come up with some way to trick him,' said the smart hare.

The hare was a soft, gentle animal. He was not the fastest in the forest, nor was he the strongest. He simply relied on his wit to protect himself. He had been dealing with animals much bigger and stronger than him his whole life.

The hare's words gave the animals hope. They began to plan earnestly, debating and arguing amongst themselves.

When they finally had a plan they were all confident about they decided to approach the lion. A small group of animals went to the den that was the lion's home to let him know of their deal.

'What is all this?' the lion's voice boomed. 'It seems the hunt has come to me today!' The lion laughed, his deep voice sending shivers down the animals' spines.

The bear who had come with the animals stepped forward. He took a deep breath before saying, 'Mr Lion, we have an offer for you. The way you are hunting every day, soon there will be no animals left in this forest at all.'

The lion scoffed. 'Who are you to tell me how to hunt? I am the most powerful animal in all the land. Do not question

me, or I will make sure to eat you next.'

'We would never dare to question you! We only come with an offer. Every day, we will bring you one animal for your meal. This way you will have steady food coming to you for many years.'

This offer pleased the lion. He enjoyed the thought of food being delivered to him every day. It made him feel important and respected. He stood tall and peered down at the trembling animals. Yes, he liked this a lot.

'I accept your offer. You must remember, however, that if you fail to send someone for even a single day I will not hesitate to hunt everyone I see fit.'

'Of course,' said the relieved bear. 'We will not fail you!'

Their mission successful, the animals turned around and walked back to the safety of their homes as fast as possible. Their plan was in motion.

The next day the hare set off for the lion's den. No one would be able to tell from looking at him that he was off to be someone's meal. He looked happy and cheerful.

The lion was waiting impatiently. When he saw the hare approaching, he began to roar.

'What is this? I have been waiting all morning and all I get is this small hare? Just wait, I'm going to hunt every animal in this forest and teach them a lesson!'

'Please wait! I promise, this is not what it looks like!' the hare cried. 'There were four more hares sent with me to satisfy your hunger. Only, we ran into a most ferocious beast who devoured my companions! I barely managed to escape to be able to reach you.'

The lion was not happy to hear this. 'What ferocious beast? Who would dare to eat my meal?' he demanded.

'Have you not seen him?' the hare asked. 'He is the strongest animal there is. His roar is like nothing you have ever heard, and he can take down any number of animals.'

The lion was angry. Was this hare suggesting that there was a beast who could take him on in a fight? He was the strongest animal there was!

'Where was this ferocious beast? Take me to him,' the lion roared. 'I will teach him what happens to anyone who dares to take what is mine!'

So the hare and the lion set of. The hare led the lion to an old well near the edge of the forest. It had been abandoned many years ago and not many people knew about it anymore. The hare pointed to it, saying, 'That is where he lives, Mr Lion. Look into the well and see for yourself.'

The lion leaned into the well and came face to face with another lion. It had a large, menacing teeth and a huge mane surrounding his face. It truly looked ferocious. The lion took a deep breath and roared at this strange lion with all his might. The lion in the well roared back at him, his voice much deeper, ringing in the lion's ears and making the hair on his back stand up.

Now the lion was truly upset. How dare this other lion challenge him in the forest he had claimed as his? With all his strength, he leaped into the well, determined to win this fight.

The truth was, there was no other lion at all. There was only one foolish lion who had been fighting with his own reflection. He landed in the water with a splash, trying to fight someone that did not exist. He sank into the water and by the time he realised what was happening, it was to late. He was already drowning.

Meanwhile, the clever little hare had been sitting nearby. After he saw the lion disappear into the depths of the well, he got up with a little hop and made his way back home, knowing that all the animals in the forest were safe once more.

25. THE MONKEY AND THE CROCODILE

On a mango tree by the river lived a little monkey. He was the happiest monkey in all the land, because he got to eat mangoes in the shade as long as summer lasted.

Across the riverbank lived a crocodile. The sight of the monkey enjoying his mangoes tempted him. Eventually he gathered the courage to float towards the monkey's tree and ask if he could try some rich and tasty mangoes as well.

'Of course! There's enough for us both,' replied the monkey. He threw down a ripe mango and the crocodile caught it in his mouth. It was sweet and juicy. Flavour exploded in the crocodile's mouth.

Sharing mangoes is a special thing. Soon, the crocodile began to visit every day, and the two friends would spend many hours talking about everything they could possibly think of as they shared the delicious fruit. They became the best of friends.

The crocodile would go home and tell his wife all about the generous monkey and his incredible mangoes, and as the days went by, she began to get jealous. She too wanted a taste of these mangoes! She too wanted to spend hours talking to her husband in the sun.

As she heard more about the monkey and his generosity, her thoughts shifted to his heart. How sweet must be the heart of someone so good. Someone who ate such luscious things every day. She began to drool just thinking about it. She decided to mention it to her husband.

'Don't you think because of all the sweet mangoes he eats, the monkey will be sweeter than anything we have ever tried?' she asked one day.

'I ... don't know,' the crocodile said, confused.

'Think about it! He spends all day eating perfectly ripe, juicy mangoes and is always kind and good to you. It can only mean that he has the sweetest heart ever.'

'I guess. I've just never thought about it,' the crocodile replied.

'Really? It might be the best thing we have ever eaten,' she tempted him.

This made the crocodile uncomfortable. The monkey had brought joy in his life. To think about eating him was unimaginable. How dare his wife even say such a thing! He firmly refused to talk about this for even a moment more.

But the crocodile's wife was restless. The crocodile went out and ate whatever he wanted, so why shouldn't she? As the days went by, a plan began to form in her mind.

One evening, when the crocodile was returning from yet another day of sharing mangoes with the monkey, she pretended to be sick.

'There's nothing that can cure me,' she told the crocodile.

The crocodile was worried. 'There must be something that will work? Please, tell me, I will do anything,' he said.

'Anything? Are you sure?'

'Yes, yes! Please, I will do whatever it takes to make you well.'

'Okay. The doctor said that a monkey's heart, the sweetest you can find, is the only thing that will cure me,' she said in a pained voice.

The crocodile was shocked. He didn't know what to say.

'But I knew that would be too difficult. I told you, there is nothing that can be done!' the wife said, beginning to cry softly.

This shook the crocodile. 'No, no,' he insisted, he would do it and make sure that his wife's health was well again. Promising to come back with the monkey's heart, he began to swim towards the mango tree—the place he had spent so many lovely afternoons.

When he reached, he called out to the monkey, who appeared from behind the branches, happy to see his friend again.

'Hello,' he cried, waving from his tree. 'How lucky I am to see you twice today!'

'Yes,' the crocodile said, 'I came back because my wife has invited you over for dinner. You see, she has heard so much about you and really wants to meet you.'

The monkey was overjoyed. A dinner invitation! No one had ever called him home before. He accepted, beginning to get down from his tree. Reaching the water's edge, he paused.

'I'm so sorry, but I cannot swim. I don't know how I will cross the river to get to your home,' the monkey said.

'Oh, that's no problem at all,' the crocodile replied a little nervously. 'I'll take you on my back. Just jump on.'

Once the monkey was nicely settled on his back, the crocodile began to swim across the river. The monkey was excited. He wondered what kind of food had been prepared for dinner—what it would be like to meet a new crocodile. But soon he was confused, because once they reached the middle of the river, the crocodile stopped.

Just as the monkey was about to ask what had happened, he noticed with alarm that they were beginning to sink!

'What are you doing,' he cried, 'I can't breathe underwater!'

Hearing the fear in the monkey's voice, the crocodile couldn't keep lying. Ashamed and nervous, he confessed everything. That his wife was sick, and a monkey's heart was the only thing that could cure her. 'What was I supposed to do,' he begged the monkey to understand.

The monkey, besides being generous and kind, was also smart. He understood that the crocodile had been fooled by his wife's greed.

As he sat on the crocodile's back, in the middle of the river, his heart beating very fast, he tried to think of a way to save himself.

'Oh, you should have said you wanted my heart in the beginning! Now we have to go all the way back to get it,' he said.

Confused, the crocodile asked what that meant. Patiently, the monkey explained that he actually kept his heart tucked away inside the tree, to keep it safe. If the crocodile had told him that's what his wife wanted, he would have brought it with him.

Relieved, the crocodile turned back and began to swim towards the tree. As soon as they were close, the monkey leaped off his back and into the safety of the branches, high up in the mango tree.

'You fool,' he said to the crocodile. 'No one can survive with their heart outside their body. Not only has your wife lost her dinner, you have also lost a friend forever. Don't come back to my tree ever again. Tell your wife that she has the most foolish husband, who got tricked twice today.'